To Nicole
Best Wishes
C Stevens

Grey Cat At Sea

by Joan Skogan
Illustrated by Claudia Stewart

This book is for the REKIN, for Joe and Shane, and for a grey cat called Cape James and a black cat called Bill. Both cats lived on boats. - J.S.

To Veronika and to my parents. - C.S.

POLESTAR
BOOK PUBLISHERS

Some cats must search in many places to find a home. One cat went to sea to search.

Small and grey and lonely, she sat on Ballantyne Pier in Vancouver harbour and cried. A Polish sailor called Henryk heard her and thought of his own cat, safe and warm at home in Poland. He put the grey kitten into his pocket and walked up the gangplank onto his ship.

The ship sailed. As she steamed under Lion's Gate Bridge, Henryk and his shipmates looked back at Vancouver harbour. They would not see Ballantyne Pier, or set foot on land again, until spring, and then summer, had turned to fall.

The grey kitten did not look back. She did not care about leaving the land behind. She was already looking at the ropes coiled on the ship's deck, and the life rings hanging from the rails. Lifting her paws carefully, she stepped over a knife left lying under a wooden bench. She sniffed at nets that smelled like fish.

The grey kitten was sailing on a Polish factory trawler named REKIN, which means "shark." REKIN was bound for the hake fishing grounds in the deep waters off the west coast of Vancouver Island. The grey kitten did not care when the captain sighted Amphritrite Point light and ordered the helmsman to turn westward to the open sea. She cared about her new home on REKIN's trawl deck.

On the trawl deck, the only food for a kitten was hake. Henryk set out water in a jar lid and milk on Sundays. The grey kitten slept on the shelf beside the kettle in the deck crew's crowded tea room while their blue-checked shirts and work gloves danced on drying lines above her.

When the captain's voice boomed down from the bridge, the grey kitten hid under the wooden bench on the port side of the trawl deck. "Wydajemy!" the captain called, "Shoot the net!" From under the bench, the grey kitten watched as the fishermen worked the winches to send the huge trawl net down REKIN's stern ramp into the sea.

While the net was in the water, the trawl bosun made a monkey's fist knot for the grey kitten to roll on deck. Henryk let her sit on his shoulder while he sharpened his knives, and the other fishermen dangled scraps of net twine for her to chase.

"Wybieramy!" the captain called, "Haul the net!" Slowly, slowly, the net full of hake was winched back on board. Under the bench, the grey kitten's ears twitched as sea gulls screamed and the bosun whistled signals to his crew. When she heard the slap, slap, slap sound of fish sliding into the tanks, she poked her nose out from beneath the bench.

The grey kitten did not care about the tons of hake sliding down to the filleting machines and freezers below decks. She cared about the one hake Henryk threw under the bench for her every haul.

The grey kitten was happy living on the trawl deck. The sun shone and the ship rolled and swayed, but the sea did not come on deck. The kitten grew a little bigger.

One day, everything changed. The rain poured down. The wind blew hard and REKIN rolled heavily in the waves. The sea came onto the deck and the door to the fishermen's tea room was closed. The grey kitten sat on the deck and cried.

A Canadian woman called Joanna tucked her inside her rain jacket. Joanna's job on REKIN was to count the catch and make sure everyone on board knew the Canadian fishing regulations.

The grey kitten did not care about Joanna's job. She cared about finding a new home.

Joanna carried the kitten up three decks to the bridge and put her down in the captain's chair. The captain came out of his chart room and frowned. He did not want a kitten living on his bridge.

The grey kitten did not care what the captain wanted. A home on the bridge was better than a home on the trawl deck. The rain and the sea did not come onto the bridge. There was no need to hide under a wooden bench when the net went down into the sea or was hauled back. The grey kitten curled herself around the radar hood and slept.

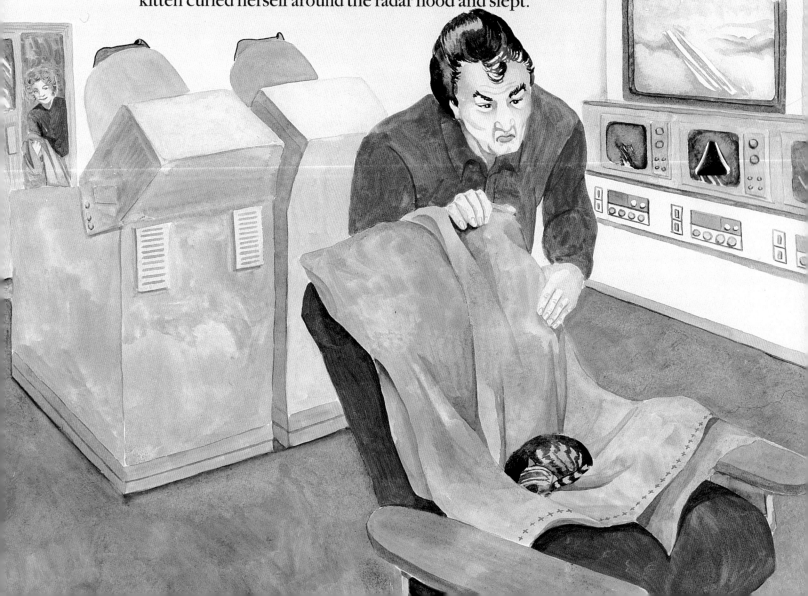

When Joanna finished her work on REKIN, the ship sailed closer to land. Joanna climbed down a rope ladder and jumped into the little boat which would take her ashore. The captain and Henryk and the trawl bosun and the deck crew waved goodbye. Joanna waved back.

The grey kitten did not care that Joanna was gone from the ship. She was happy in her new home on the bridge. During the day watch on the bridge, the captain stroked the grey kitten while he looked into his radar. He let her sit on his shoulder while he searched the sounder screen for hake schools. The third officer cut up sausages for her and gave her milk from the officer's mess in a glass saucer every day.

On the night watch, the first officer let the grey kitten sit in the captain's chair by the window over the bow. The second officer carried her from one side of the bridge to the other, showing her the running lights of other Polish ships – DELFIN, the dolphin, and WLOCZNIK, the swordfish, along with ANTARES and INDUS and ARCTURUS, named after stars.

The grey kitten grew to be a small cat. The captain and his officers called her Szara Kotka, which means "grey cat."

By early fall, REKIN's cargo holds were full of frozen fish. The ship steamed in from open waters, bound for port in Vancouver.

Grey Cat did not care when the captain sighted Amphritrite Point light again and ordered the helmsman to turn south. She was asleep, curled around the radar hood.

The captain looked down at her. He and his crew were flying home to Poland. A new captain and crew were coming to take REKIN to the Bering Sea. They might not understand that the bridge was Grey Cat's home. Grey Cat might walk down the gangplank onto Ballantyne Pier and not find her way back. Grey Cat was a shipmate. Shipmates look after each other.

The captain told his radio officer to send a telegram to Joanna in Vancouver. The telegram said,

"Come to Ballantyne Pier and pick up small member of crew.

Regards,
Captain on REKIN."

Joanna brought a small box to Ballantyne Pier. The captain, the first officer, the second officer and the third officer worked together to catch Grey Cat and put her into the box. Henryk came up from the trawl deck to tie the box with twine and carry it to Joanna's car.

Inside the box, Grey Cat scratched and hissed. She was angry about leaving her home on the bridge. She missed the roll and sway of the ship and the rumble of the main engines. She was frightened by the strange steadiness of land, and the stop-and-start sound of the car engine.

Joanna opened the box when she got home, but Grey Cat did not come out even when Joanna put a dish of catfood on the floor for her.

Grey Cat did not care about catfood. She wanted Polish sausage or hake. She wanted her home on the bridge and her sleeping place by the radar.

Joanna carried Grey Cat outside and set her down in the grass under the apple tree. Grey Cat did not care about the grass or the apple tree. She wanted the sea.

She crept back into Joanna's house and hid in the dark under the spare bed. "Szara Kotka," Joanna called, but Grey Cat did not move. Her home on the sea was gone and there was only the darkness under the bed.

Joanna's son, Joe, came to visit her. He crawled under the spare bed and reached for Grey Cat, then he stroked her while she sniffed at him. Joe lived on his gillnet boat up the coast. He smelled like a fisherman.

Joe carried Grey Cat outside and put her down on the grass. He climbed the apple tree while she watched. Grey Cat ran up the tree after him, then down again, and around and around on the grass. Joe climbed down and put her on his shoulder. He took a net knife from his back pocket and unwound some twine for her to chase.

When Joe was visiting, Grey Cat was happy in her home on shore. She ate catfood. She slept on the spare bed with Joe until he went back to his home on the boat.

Grey Cat looked for him everywhere. When she could not find him in the house or by the apple tree, she walked up and down the busy street calling him.

Joanna knew Grey Cat could get lost or hurt on the street, so she kept her in the house. Grey Cat hid in the darkness under the spare bed again. She did not care about a home on shore anymore.

One day in the spring, when Grey Cat was nearly a year old, Joanna put her into a cardboard box. Grey Cat did not care. Joanna put the box into her car and drove through Vancouver and across Lion's Gate Bridge. She drove onto the ferry at Horseshoe Bay. Grey Cat heard the faint rumble of the ferry's main engines and she felt the roll and the sway of the sea. Inside the box, she made no sound.

When the ferry docked in Nanaimo, Joanna drove north. Grey Cat heard the stop-and-start sound of the car engine again and she clawed her way out of the box. She howled. She crawled under the car seat. She climbed on top of Joanna's head. She did not care about anything except getting out of the car.

After a long time, Joanna and Grey Cat came to the fishermen's dock in Kelsey Bay. Joanna tucked Grey Cat inside her coat and walked down the ramp and along the dock until she came to a small gillnetter named ALERT BAY. She stepped on board.

Joe came out of the gillnetter's cabin and Grey Cat jumped down from Joanna's arms. She sniffed at Joe to make sure he was the same Joe. She looked through the galley door into the cabin and saw a spare bunk with an old green sleeping bag on it.

The ALERT BAY rolled and swayed. Grey Cat crossed the deck and looked into the empty fish hatch. Joe flipped a herring out of a bucket. Grey Cat ate the herring. She stepped over the door sill into the cabin and leapt up onto the spare bunk. She pawed at the green sleeping bag until it was arranged the way she wanted it. She lay down and purred.

Grey Cat was home.

GLOSSARY

bosun: the person in charge of the fishermen on the deck crew and the trawl nets. Also called "deck boss."

bow: the forward end of the ship.

factory trawler: a large ship with a factory below decks where the fish caught in the trawl are headed and gutted or filletted, then frozen.

galley: the kitchen on a boat. The galley and the mess are often the same room.

gangplank: a moveable plank or metal walkway used as a bridge for walking onto a ship.

gillnetter: a small fishing boat using nets that catch fish, usually salmon or herring, by their gills.

hake: a saltwater fish in the cod family.

helmsman: the person who steers a ship.

mess: the place where meals are eaten on a ship.

depth sounder: a device which shows the depth and features of the ocean floor, and indicates the presence of schools of fish.

radar: a device which uses reflected radio waves to show nearby boats as points on the radar screen at night or in fog.

radar hood: a black rubber eye shield attached to the radar screen.

stern: the rear end of a ship.

port side: the left side of the ship, looking forward. Starboard is the right side.

running lights: the lights used at night on a moving ship.

trawling: catching fish by towing a bag-shaped net behind the boat. Hake are trawled at mid-water depth, 50 metres or more beneath the sea surface in deep water.

Published by
Polestar Press, Ltd., P.O. Box 69382, Station K, Vancouver, B.C., V5K 4W6

Distributed by
Raincoast Books Distribution Ltd., 112 East 3rd Avenue,
Vancouver, B.C., V5T 1C8, 604-873-6581

Canadian Cataloguing in Publication Data
Skogan, Joan, 1945-
Grey cat at sea
ISBN 0-919591-69-8
I. Stewart, Claudia. II. Title.
PS8587.K63G7 1991   jC813'.54   C91-091503-2
PZ7.S563Gr 1991

Acknowledgements
Published with the assistance of the Canada Council and the B.C. Cultural Services Branch

Printed in Hong Kong.

Cover design by Jim Brennan